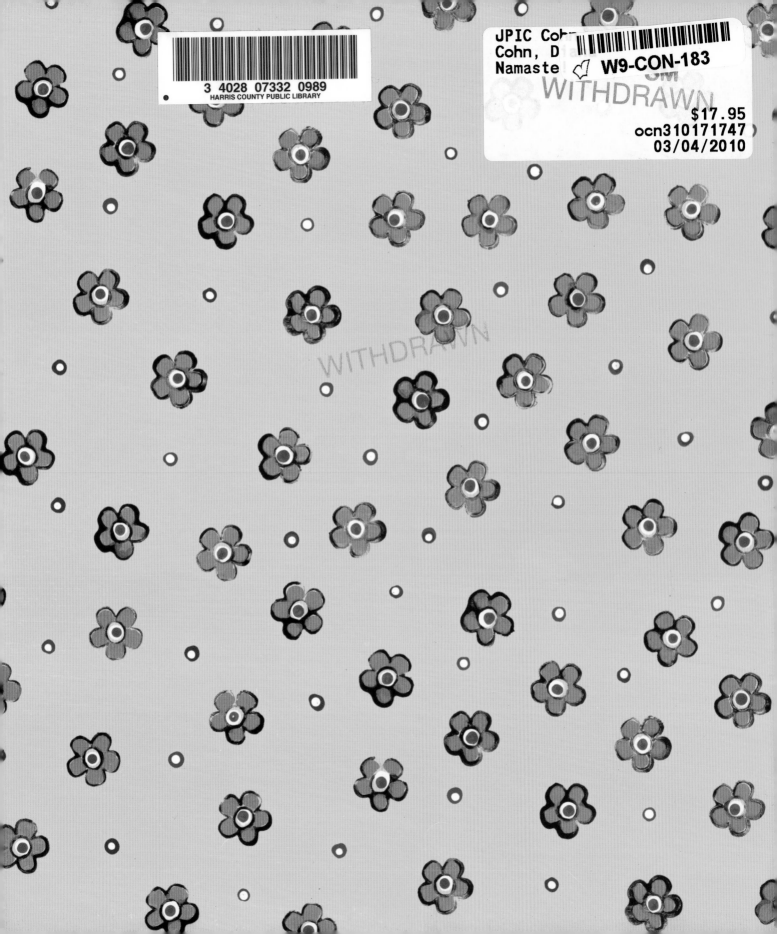

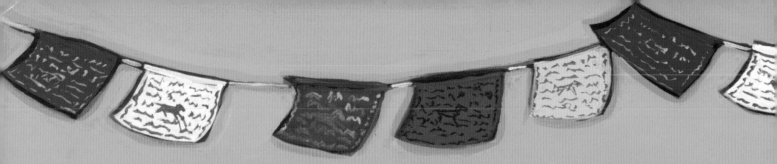

Library of Congress Cataloging-in-Publication Data

Cohn, Diana.
  Namaste! / by Diana Cohn ; illustrated by Amy
Córdova ; with an Afterword by Ang Rita Sherpa
of the Mountain Institute.
     p. cm.
  Summary: Whenever Nima meets someone on her
long walk to the village market in Nepal, she brings
her hands together with her fingers almost touching
her chin, bows her head slightly, and says "Namaste,"
which means "the light in me meets the light in you."
Includes information on the geography, culture, and
people of Nepal.
     ISBN 978-0-88010-625-2
[1. Salutations –Fiction. 2. Sherpa (Nepalese people)–
Fiction. 3. Conduct of life –Fiction. 4. Spiritual life–
Fiction. 5. Nepal–Fiction.] I. Córdova, Amy, ill.
II. Sherpa, Ang Rita. III. Title.
     PZ7.C6649Nam 2009
[E] –dc22

          2009003216

SteinerBooks
610 Main Street, Great Barrington, MA 01230

www.steinerbooks.org

Namaste (pronounced nah-mah-stay) literally means
"I bow to you." It is generally translated as "the light
in me meets the light in you."

DEDICATION

To Sir Edmund Hillary and Tenzing Norgay

To my goddaughter Juliette Allayaud, and for those who practice
an understanding of "namaste" everyday in their relations with others
and in their teachings – Peggy Orr, Nikki Estrada, Lisa Schubert,
Kewulay Kamara, Gene Gollogly, Paul Winter, and Kevin and Erin
Maile O'Keefe – and to my extended family in Kathmandu, Nepal –
Anjana, Purna, Prajwol, and Siddhartha Shakya – and for Ellen Coon
and Ted Riccardi who introduced me to this special part of the world. – D.C.

To all those who helped make NAMASTE! come into being and to loving
kindness – may it find its home in each and every heart in this our one,
precious world. – A.C.

To the memories of my father-in-law, Mr. Pasang Kami (PK) Sherpa
and to my father, Mr. Mingma Tsering Sherpa, whose lives have been an
inspiration to me and my family and have provided me with incredible
support. – A.R.S.

Namaste!

by Diana Cohn
illustrated by Amy Córdova

Afterword by Ang Rita Sherpa

SteinerBooks

nima Sherpa lives at the top of the world, where the tallest mountain on earth, Chomolongma, towers above the clouds.

On the roof of Nima's house, yellow, green, red, white, and blue prayer flags flutter and flap in the early morning winds. Down the hillside the Milk River rushes, white with cold.

Every year, Nima's father leaves home to work as a mountain guide.
Although he is gone just a few weeks, for Nima it feels as if a whole

Nima and her mother light some incense and offer blessings for her
father's journey. Although he always knows when a storm is coming,

Then, Nima gets ready for the long walk to the market village where she goes to school. Every day, she passes dozens of people on her way. When she sees them, she brings her hands together with her fingers almost touching her chin,

bows her head slightly, and says *Namaste!* "*Namaste* means *the light in me meets the light in you,*" Nima's mother tells her. "When you say *Namaste!* try to see the special spark of light that shines within every person's heart."

As Nima walks along, she meets some porters carrying big baskets of biscuits and tea and pots and pans of all sizes. She remembers her father's stories about helping people. Maybe the story she will tell him will be about how she helps others too.

But Nima is too little to carry such a heavy load. Can she find another way to help them? Nima calls out *Namaste!* The porters are very tired, but when they see Nima, each one smiles and returns her greeting, *Namaste!*

Soon Nima hears a silvery *ching-sing-sing, ching-sing-sing* behind her. The bells ring and ring from a caravan of yaks and naks that weaves its way up and down the meandering trail.

Nima waits patiently at the side of the dusty road. *Namaste! she says
quietly to her animal friends as they clamor past.*

As Nima skips along, she sees a group of travelers looking at a stupa by the side of the road. She wonders how she can help them? She doesn't understand what they are saying, so she simply greets them with *Namaste!*

The travelers smile at Nima, and bring their hands together and bow their heads, just as she does. *Namaste!* they all say together.

After school, Nima sees her father's friend Tenzing, a Tibetan trader. He is sitting in the marketplace among the other traders who have walked many weeks over the high mountains to sell and trade salt and butter, jewelry

and fabrics, and other wares. Tenzing trades his carved bone bowls for some jars filled with honey. *Namaste!* Nima shouts. Tenzing's smile breaks across his broad face like the rays of the sun streaming through a cloud. *Namaste!* he says

Tenzing motions for Nima to sit beside him and offers her a spoonful of the golden honey. "Nima, you are full of sweetness and light, just like this honey." Nima smiles at her old friend. "Thank you, Tenzing," she says

savoring the treat. "And," says Tensing, "you brighten my day every time you share that sweetness and light, every time you say *Namaste!*"

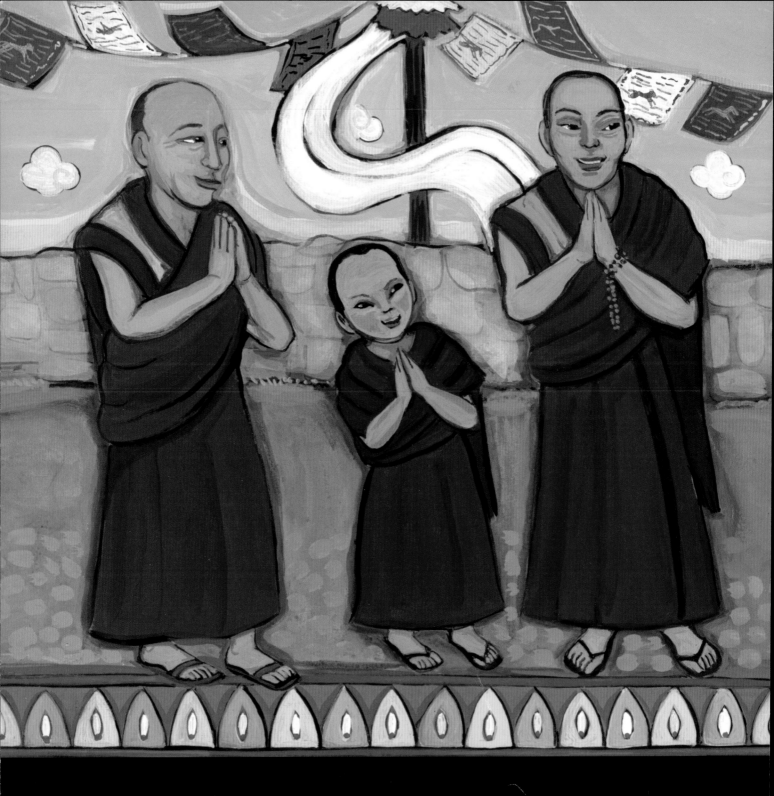

On her way home, Nima shares her sweetness and light with every *Namaste!* she says . . . with monks on their way to their monasteries . . . with porters carrying their goods to market . . . with travelers trekking to their next lodge

Nima will have a story for her father when he returns home.
She will tell him how she helps others every time she says *Namaste!*

The light in me

meets the *light* in you.

GLOSSARY

Chomolongma – is the Tibetan and Sherpa name for the tallest mountain in the world. It means "Mother Goddess of the Earth." In the Nepali language, it is called "Sagarmatha," which means "forehead in the sky." In the West this mountain is well known as Mount Everest.

Khata – is a ceremonial cloth that is draped around a person's neck like a scarf, and is given as an offering and for good luck. It is often presented as a gift at festive occasions. Khatas are usually made of white or yellow silk.

Namaste – (pronounced nah-mah-stay) literally means "I bow to you." It is generally translated as "the light in me meets the light in you." When spoken to another person, it is commonly accompanied by a slight bow. The gesture is made with the hands pressed together, palms touching and fingers pointed upward, in front of the chest. The greeting Namaste represents the belief that there is a Divine spark within each of us. The gesture without words carries the same meaning.

Nima – means "Sun." It is traditional for the Sherpas to give a child the name of the day on which he or she was born, and so Nima's name indicates that she was born on a Sunday.

Prayer flags – Tibetans consider prayer flags to be holy. Prayer flags are hung in the open – outside temples and holy sites, strung across bridges, rooftops, and mountain passes – where the flags can meet the wind. The Tibetans believe that when the flags are blown by the wind the prayers printed on the flags will spread good will, peace, and compassion to all. The five colors of the prayer flags represent the elements:

Blue	–	sky/space
White	–	air/wind
Red	–	fire
Green	–	water
Yellow	–	earth

Sherpa – means "people from the east." Sherpas are an ethnic group who live in Nepal and are known worldwide for their great skill as mountain climbers, guides, and traders.

Stupa – A mound-like structure that contains holy objects or relics. It is one of the most ancient forms of Buddhist art. Stupas are the most numerous monuments in Buddhist areas and are designed with deep symbolism and sacred geometry to emanate blessings and peace.

Tenzing – is a common Tibetan name that means "holder of the teachings" or "bearer of wisdom."

Tiger-riding goddess – The Tibetans believe that their mountains are sacred and are protected by gods and goddesses. Chomolongma is protected by Jomo Miyo-Lang-Sangma, a goddess often depicted riding on a tiger and holding a bowl of tsampa.

Tsampa – This porridge made from barley flour and mixed with salty, yak butter tea is a staple food in Sherpa households.

Yak and nak (male and female of the species) – These high altitude animals provide hide for leather, milk for dairy products, meat, wool for clothing, and dung for fuel and fertilizer. Tibetan traders use these animals to carry products from village to village, transporting their goods over great distances and high mountain passes.

AFTERWORD

Ang Rita Sherpa

Nepal

About 29 million people live in Nepal. Although Nepali is the official language, most of the ethnic groups who live in the different regions of this country have their own languages, lifestyles, and customs. Religion is a deeply rooted part of Nepali life. Hinduism is the primary religion, but Buddhism and other beliefs are interwoven with many of the traditions and festivals that permeate every aspect of life in this country.

Nepal is rectangular in shape. Three geographic regions – Terai, Mountain, and Hill – run its length in three belts, corresponding roughly to elevation, from low in the south to high in the north. The Terai, in the south, is home to jungles with tigers, rhinoceroses, and elephants. The Mountain region in the north includes the Himalayas.

The Himalayas

The world's highest mountains are located in Asia. The Himalaya Mountain Range is still rising, and its peaks have not yet been worn down as have older mountain chains. Eight of the tallest mountains in the world are part of the Himalayas: Everest, Kanchenjunga, Lhotse, Makalu, Cho Oyu, Dhanlagiri, Manaslu, and Annapurna.

This area is refuge for many threatened and endangered wildlife species, including the snow leopard, musk deer, red panda, and Himalayan black bear. Scores of rhododendron and orchid species are visited by over 300 bird species.

The Sherpa People

The Sherpas are Nepal's best-known ethnic group. Bringing their Tibetan Buddhist traditions and culture, they migrated from eastern Tibet and settled in the rugged mountain valleys in the Khumbu region of northeastern Nepal over 500 years ago.

Sherpa food is limited to crops that can grow at high altitudes. Potatoes, buckwheat, and barley are the traditional main foods in the Khumbu region. Sherpas also grow turnips and greens and make dairy products such as butter, yogurt and cheese from the milk of their yaks. Tibetan traders travel with yak caravans over the high passes of the Himalayas to sell salt and dried meat in the Sherpa markets.

Sir Edmund Hillary and Tenzing Norgay

On May 29, 1953, the New Zealand mountaineer Sir Edmund Hillary along with mountaineer Sherpa Tenzing Norgay became the first climbers to reach the summit of Mount Everest. Following his ascent of Everest, Sir Edmund founded the Himalayan Trust and devoted much of the rest of his life to helping the Sherpa people of Nepal. Through his efforts many schools and hospitals were built in the Solo Khumbu region of the Himalayas.

The accomplishment of climbing Mount Everest inspired many visitors to come see the tallest mountain in the world. Rising tourism brought new jobs and opportunities for the Sherpa people, but also has had a damaging impact on this remote and fragile environment. Thanks to the work of Sir Edmund and others, in 1976 Sagarmatha National Park was established to protect this very special place. In 1979, the region was declared a World Heritage Natural Site in recognition of its unique ecology and the cultural heritage of the Sherpa people.

Preserving Mountain Cultures

Many people and organizations care deeply for this part of the world and are dedicated to safeguarding its beauty and cultures. One organization working to preserve mountain cultures all over the world, including in the Himalayan region, is The Mountain Institute (TMI), founded in 1972. Based in Washington, DC, TMI has offices and community-based programs in the Andean, Appalachian, and Himalayan mountain ranges that empower communities living in some of the world's most remote and rugged regions to protect their environments while enhancing their livelihoods.

Mountain people themselves live close to the land, and their farming, grazing, hunting and woodcutting maintain a delicate balance between sustainability and destruction. But mountains, often in the world's "hot spots" of biodiversity, are rich in timber, water, and mineral resources that attract severe development pressures to fragile areas. The growing lure and accessibility of mountains as tourist destinations also places strains on infrastructure and ecosystems. To minimize these effects, TMI works in partnership with other organizations to create effective means of conserving the unique mountain ecosystems and species.

* * * * *

The creators of this book – Diana and Amy – witnessed the work of The Mountain Institute while doing research for their book in Nepal. With deeply felt gratitude for the generosity of TMI staff in Kathmandu, they are donating a portion of the proceeds from the sale of *Namaste!* to support the Institute's critical work preserving mountain cultures in the Himalayas and around the world.

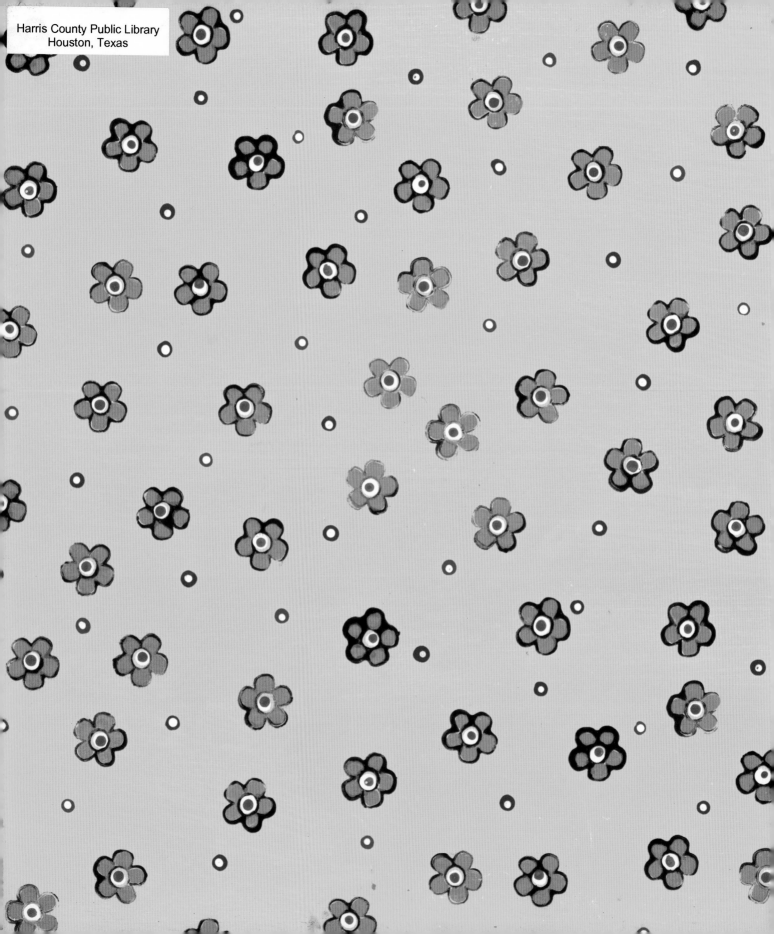